GIRLS SURVIVE

Raintree is an imprint of Capstone Global Library Limited, a company incorporated in England and Wales having its registered office at 264 Banbury Road, Oxford, OX2 7DY – Registered company number: 6695582

www.raintree.co.uk
myorders@raintree.co.uk

Designed by Kayla Rossow
Original illustrations © Capstone Global Library Limited 2022
Originated by Capstone Global Library Ltd
Printed and bound in India

978 1 3982 1488 0

British Library Cataloguing in Publication Data
A full catalogue record for this book is available from the British Library.

Acknowledgements
We would like to thank the following for permission to reproduce photographs:
Shutterstock: Spalnic (paper texture background), vtaurus (geometric background)
Author photo: Richard Jervis. Cover Art: Jane Pica

MARIA
AND THE PLAGUE
A Black Death
Survival Story

by Natasha Deen

illustrated by Francesca Ficorilli

raintree 🍃

a Capstone company — publishers for children

CHAPTER ONE

---

13 April 1347
Florence, Italy

The chill from the rainy morning settled on my shoulders as I left my house. The sun hadn't risen yet, but I needed to get to the grain market. Papa and my seventeen-year-old brother, Paolo, worked as labourers for the wool guild, Arte della Lana. They were counting on me to get bread for the family.

Getting food was hard. The last few years had tested all of us in Florence. Earthquakes, along with the rain, had led to food shortages and forced our family to leave our farm. We moved to Florence two years ago. My family had hoped for a better life in the city. I fought back the tears and tried not to think of last year. That was when Mamma and my newborn sister, Flora, had died. Their bodies just couldn't keep going with so little food.

I walked faster, hoping to outrun the memory of burying them. But I heard the echo of the priest's prayers in my ears. Soon I was running from the pain. The mud splashed my legs. No matter how fast I ran, I couldn't outrun my broken heart. My tears mixed with the rain. I wiped them away. I reminded myself that I still had Papa, Nonna, Joseph and my big brother.

As I got closer to the city centre, I slowed to catch my breath. The roads were filling with people. I used to love how crowded and lively the streets were. But now people were starving and scared.

The city was trying to help its citizens by rationing bread, but the food shortages made people dangerous. Last week, when I was queuing for bread, two people behind me started arguing over who got there first. Their raised voices turned into blows. That's what it was like now – neighbours fighting. I turned the corner, thinking I would be one of the first in the queue for the day's ration. I thought wrong.

The queue snaked down the street. People in front of me grumbled. The sound reminded me of the rumble of an empty belly. My stomach growled too, but I ignored it. The rain stopped as I got there. I hoped there would be bread, not just for me, Papa and Paolo, but also for Joseph and Nonna too.

Nonna was old and sick. The bread would be key to her chance of surviving. I had to get bread so I could share with her and Joseph. I worried Nonna wouldn't make it through to next spring.

The queue moved slowly. I hoped I wouldn't hear anyone cry out, "The bread is gone!"

More people joined the queue. At twelve years old, I was small for my age. People pushed me, and I pushed back so they wouldn't take my place. I paid attention to people's moods. I didn't want to get caught in any fights.

"Maria! Maria Rosso!" a voice cried from somewhere behind me.

I turned. Even with the crowd, it was easy to spot Joseph. He was tall, skinny and had black hair. He ran to me.

"Hey!" the short man behind me said, shoving Joseph.

A flash of anger went through me. My hands tightened into fists.

"Get to the back of the queue," said the man. "Wait your turn."

"I'm not here for bread," Joseph told him.

"Good!" The man spat next to Joseph's feet, then shook his fist in Joseph's face. "I haven't eaten in two days. If you try to push ahead, I'll stop you."

We watched to see if the man would make more trouble, but he turned away. I slowly exhaled. Joseph stepped towards me.

"If you *are* here for bread," I told him, "you need to get to the back."

Joseph shook his head and whispered, "I already have my bread."

I was glad because it meant we wouldn't need to share my loaf.

"Did you talk to your father about getting a job?" Joseph asked.

"Yes," I said, "but Papa said he wants me to stay at home. He says the work I do there is important." I kicked at the dirt. "If we were still on our farm, I could've helped with the crops or the animals. I feel useless here."

"You're not useless," said Joseph. "Taking care of the household is important work."

I shrugged. *That may be true*, I thought, *but our family needs money*. "At least you have a job that pays money," I said.

Joseph scowled. "It doesn't pay enough, and I can't stand how badly the men treat me." He glanced my way. "I want to find another job."

My heart clenched. "You mean the ships, don't you?"

"I can make more money with them than working as a carder for the wool guild," said Joseph.

"That's not certain," I said.

Joseph toed the ground. "It would be more exciting, that's for certain."

"But you're all that Nonna has left. She would be sad if you were gone," I said. *I would too*, I thought, but I didn't say it. I knew Joseph already felt guilty about wanting to leave Florence. I didn't want to make him feel worse.

"Nonna and I lost everyone – Mamma, Papa, my brothers and sisters. If I'm to take care of Nonna, I need a better job," he said. "This bread is the only thing we have to eat, except for the weeds and grass."

Joseph and Nonna weren't the only ones eating grass and weeds. Sometimes, my family and I did too. I couldn't believe how terrible things had become for the people of Florence.

"What about the Silk Road?" I asked. "What if you became a trader?" Joseph loved the ocean and wanted to be a sailor. But being a trader meant we would see him more often.

"I want to be on the ocean," said Joseph. "I want to sail to different lands."

I tried to keep the sadness out of my voice. "But you'd be so far away," I said.

"I know," Joseph said softly. "I would miss you, Maria. But we have to take care of ourselves and our families, even if that means making tough choices."

Joseph and I fell silent, lost in thoughts for our families. When I got to the front of the queue, I put the bread in my bag and hurried home.

I couldn't blame Joseph for wanting to do anything he could to help Nonna. I wanted to do anything I could to help my family. Papa was getting older. I needed to help take care of him. When Papa got home tonight, I would tell him that I was going to get work. Joseph was right. We had to take care of ourselves.

I was so focused on planning how I would talk to Papa, I stopped paying attention to my surroundings. From the corner of my eye, I spotted a shadowy figure. Suddenly, someone grabbed me and pulled me into the dark alley.

It was the man from the bread queue.

"Give me your food!" he shouted. He wrenched my arm and grabbed for my bag.

I kicked him, hard, and ran. As I sped away, I heard his heavy steps pounding after me.

CHAPTER TWO

I rubbed my shoulder to ease the pain. It had been nine months since the man had pulled me into the alley and tried to steal my food. Sometimes, my arm still hurt. I had fought him off. But he'd twisted my arm hard and sometimes it still hurt.

A knock at our door interrupted the argument Papa and Paolo were having.

"I'll get it," said Paolo as I pulled my shawl close.

"Good, a visitor," grumbled Papa. "Maybe now, my children will talk about something else."

"We talk, but you don't listen," said Paolo. "We can't stay here in Florence, Papa. There's no food or money."

"Where do you think we can go?" Papa asked. "Do you think food and money will magically appear? Here, we have jobs and a home. We're staying."

I huffed, angry at Papa. I'd been begging him to let me work for months. Every time we talked, he said, "No, no, no."

I watched my brother walk across the room. He used to be thick and strong. Now, he was as thin as a scarecrow. He always made sure I ate, even if it meant he went hungry. Why couldn't Papa see we needed food? More importantly, we needed money to buy the food! If only he would let me work . . .

Papa and Paolo argued a lot these days about jobs and leaving the city. Paolo was tired of working as a carder for the wool guild. The hours were long, and the pay was terrible. Adding to our troubles were the stories travelling from neighbour to neighbour. They told of a sickness spreading throughout Italy. It had already reached Genoa and Rome. According to some people, it had infected the whole world.

The disease was frightening. Stories said infected people bled from the nose and got black spots on their skin. Worst of all, a horrible, painful death followed. With every telling of the stories, the signs of the sickness got worse and worse. It was hard to know what to believe. There were even rumours of a ship of sailors, all of whom had the disease. The sailors went from port to port, begging to dock. But they were never allowed. The fear was too great that the sailors would infect everyone in the port cities.

It didn't make sense. If the sailors had the sickness, wouldn't they have died? I had asked Papa about it, but he told me not to worry. The sickness would never come to Florence, he said. Then he changed the subject. Whenever Paolo spoke of it, Papa would glare at him and tell him to talk of something else.

Paolo opened the door. It was Joseph! The late-afternoon air blew in and chilled my skin.

"Eh, runt, why are you here?" Paolo asked as Joseph stepped inside. My brother smiled and playfully shoved him.

Joseph grinned and pushed back.

"Joseph," said Papa from his spot at the table, "how is Nonna? Do you need our help?"

"Nonna is well, thank you," Joseph said. "And yes, I do need your help. That's why I'm here."

"Oh," Papa said, raising his eyebrows. "What do you need?"

Joseph cleared his throat. "I want to take a job on the ships as soon as possible. But I can do it only if Nonna has someone to watch out for her."

My heart sank. "Nonna has agreed to let you get a job on the ships?" I asked.

Joseph nodded.

"Did she truly give you permission?" Papa asked.

Joseph shuffled his feet. "Well, not as yet. If you talked to her, I think–"

Papa sighed. "Life on a ship isn't all adventure."

"I need your help," said Joseph. "I can make much more money as a sailor. Money I can bring back to better care for Nonna. I will be back as often as I can. Please don't make me stay."

"He won't," said Paolo, his voice hard. "Just because Papa wants to live and die in Florence doesn't mean we all have to."

Papa glared at my brother. Then he turned to Joseph and said, "A sailor's hours are long. The work is hard and the weather can be terribly dangerous."

Joseph smiled sadly. "I know," he said. "But tell me how that is different from how I live right now."

Papa watched him for a moment and then nodded. "I will help you," he said. "I remember what it was like to be young and want adventure. We'll take care of Nonna while you're away."

"Finally! Some sense!" said Paolo. "Now, Papa, it is *our* turn. You, Maria and I must take Nonna and go to Milan."

"Enough, Paolo!" Papa shouted. His face was red. "We will stay in the city. It is where your mother and sister are buried. We are not leaving!"

The fight drained from my brother's face. "At least let me go with Joseph to look at the ships," Paolo said. "I can help him talk to the captains."

"I'm not a baby," said Joseph. "I'm a year older than Maria and old enough to make my own decisions. I can talk to the captains myself."

Paolo held up his hands and chuckled. "Fine, runt. I'll come and help you decide which ship you want to join. How's that?"

"Better," grumbled Joseph.

"I'm not a baby either," I said to Papa. "If Joseph is getting work, then so can I."

"No, no, no, *piccolina*," he said. "You can keep asking, but I will keep telling you no."

"Wealthy families are always in need of servants," I said. "I could help clean. I could make money and help us!"

"Maria, no!" Papa said. "If you work for a family, you must live with them." His eyes watered. "Please, Maria. I lost your mamma and Flora. Don't ask me to give you up, not yet. Another year, and we'll talk about it. I promise."

I wanted to argue. Our family needed money, but I didn't want to start a fight in front of Joseph. I decided to wait until Papa and I were alone.

Surely, if I took in mending and stayed at home, he couldn't say no, could he?

"It'll be dark soon," Paolo said. "If we're going to look at the ships, we should leave now."

I asked Papa if I could go too. He wasn't too happy about it, but he let me, as long as I stayed close to Paolo.

As Paolo, Joseph and I walked to the port, I noticed Paolo had a bag with him.

"What are you carrying in there?" I asked.

"I have some wool," Paolo said, opening the bag slightly. "I thought I could sell it to one of the sailors."

I gasped. "Paolo, no! You're not allowed to sell wool. That job is for the other men in the guild."

My brother frowned. "Why? Everyone works hard, from raising the sheep to turning the wool into yarn and clothing, then selling it. Why should some people make more money than others? It's not fair."

"If the guild finds out what you've done, they'll fine you," said Joseph. "Or worse, they might fire you. What will happen to your father and Maria if you lose your job? Put it away, Paolo."

For a moment, I thought my brother would argue. But then, finally, he sighed and closed the bag.

"Does Papa know what you were going to do?" I asked.

"No, and you can't tell him either." Paolo ran his hand through his hair. "You're too young to understand. Things are getting much worse in the city," he said.

"I'm not that young!" I said. "I know times are hard."

Paolo snorted. "Then you know more than our father," he said. "Papa doesn't understand. People are in trouble. We lost–" He caught his breath. "We lost Mamma and Flora. Joseph lost everyone, except for Nonna. None of that had to happen. We have to take care of ourselves, Maria."

Joseph nodded. "That's why I'm going to get a job on a ship."

I didn't know what to say, so I followed the boys in silence.

When we got to the docks, something wasn't right. The crowd of people was standing there, but they were eerily silent. They stood still, their eyes turned to the water.

"What's going on?" Paolo asked a man next to him.

The man shook his head. "I don't know," he said, looking confused. "Nothing good, I suspect."

"Stay here," Paolo said to Joseph and me. "I'm going to see what's happening." He pushed through the crowd, trying to get to the front of the dock.

Joseph and I looked at each other and then hurried after him.

"I told you to stay!" Paolo called over his shoulder.

"I told you I was old enough to make my own decisions," Joseph called back.

Paolo shook his head.

The waves pushed against the wooden piers and made them groan. There was a line of people in front of me. I couldn't see what was happening. I hopped up and down. The people were too tall, and I was too short. "Paolo, Joseph, can you tell what's going on?" I asked.

"Nothing good, just like the man said," Paolo said. "Men from the ship are rowing in. They must have been in a fight of some kind. They're moving slowly." He frowned. "Something is wrong, but I–" Fear whitened Paolo's face. "Maria, Joseph! We must go!"

"What is it?" I asked, my heart thumping in my chest. "What's going on?"

The crowd's silence suddenly burst into screams of terror.

"It's the sickness!" cried a man.

"It's the ship from Genoa!" screamed a woman.

More shouts came from all directions.

"They're trying to come on land!"

"They'll kill us all!"

Paolo grabbed me to keep me close. His grip was tight. He had Joseph in his other arm. Paolo swung away from the water's edge and shoved us back through the crowd.

"The people must be wrong!" I yelled. "Papa says the stories aren't true!"

"Keep moving!" Paolo shouted.

I held tight to my brother as people pushed and shoved. I stumbled and almost fell. Pain shot through my injured arm. Paolo steadied me before the crowd trampled me.

"Go, you two!" screamed Paolo. "Get out!"
He pushed Joseph and me – hard. "Run before the
crowd crushes you!"

I quickly looked over my shoulder, at the
frightened crowd behind me. Burning arrows were
now slicing through the air, towards the water.

"Run!" Paolo yelled, not just to Joseph and
me, but to anyone who heard him. "The men in the
rowing boats bring the sickness!"

I grabbed Joseph's arm and ran as hard as I
could.

CHAPTER **THREE**

---

30 March — 3 April 1348
Florence, Italy

It had been more than two months since the boats from Genoa had arrived, bringing the sickness to Florence. We now called the disease the Great Pestilence. Sometimes, I heard people call it the Mortality. No matter its name, it was terrifying. People weren't only getting sick. They were dying. The stories had been true, especially the parts about how horrible the deaths were.

Whenever someone died, the church bells rang. At first, they rang a few times a week. Now, they never seemed to stop. I lifted a cloth bundle onto my back and walked down the street. Along with the near-constant ringing of the bells was the crying coming from people's homes. Children were losing their parents. Parents were burying their babies. All I wanted to do was run home, climb into bed and pull the covers over my head to block the awful sounds. But I had to keep going. I had a job to do.

When our money nearly ran out, Papa had no choice but to let me take in mending. He was scared of Joseph, Paolo or me getting sick, but we couldn't afford to stop working. In my bundle was sewing I'd done for some families. I was taking the clothing back and getting more work in return.

Papa wasn't the only one who worried for us. Nonna refused to let Joseph go back to the docks. She didn't want him to leave the house, even though she needed the money his work brought in. Papa tried to calm her. He told her that doctors were working on a cure.

But every day, the bells rang. Every day, more people died. I hardly slept anymore. When I did, my dreams were filled with people who were sick and dying. In my very worst nightmares, Joseph, Papa and Paolo were taken from me.

I walked with the bundle on my back, head down. Some people I passed held handkerchiefs to their faces. Others covered their mouths with a handful of flowers. These people did it because they thought the bits of cloth and plants would keep them healthy. I wasn't sure about that. I sometimes held a bunch of flowers and weeds to my face because the air was rotten. The plants didn't hide the smell completely, but they helped.

People started leaving their dead family members in the road. They were too scared to keep them in the house. They feared the bodies would cause more sickness. I carefully picked my way past the bodies. I tried not to look at their faces. I tried not to think of all the happiness they would never feel again. I wished I could stop and say a prayer, but I'd promised Papa I wouldn't touch anyone or anything.

Just up the road, a small group of people was coming towards me. Most of them were crying. It was an early-morning funeral procession. I stopped and waited for it to pass by. So did a man and woman close to me. As the couple waited, they talked about the sickness. I tried not to listen, but I couldn't help it.

"The merchants are fleeing to the countryside," said the woman.

The man snorted. "Let them leave," he said. "There is no more room to bury anyone anymore. The graves are full."

The woman shuddered. "I heard they're burying everyone in mass graves now. I heard parents are sneaking out of their homes at night and abandoning

their children." She dropped her head and began
to weep.

The man pulled her close. "I won't abandon you,"
he promised. "We will get through this, together."

My heart hurt at the thought of children left
alone. The streets were getting more dangerous
every day. Some people believed if they prayed and
behaved well, the sickness would leave Florence.
Others thought it was the end of the world and that no
one needed to obey laws anymore. The risk of being
beaten up or having your belongings stolen grew
every day. It was why I'd promised Papa I would
always be home long before dusk.

As soon as the mourners were gone, I continued
on my way. People in every house where I returned
mending wanted to talk with me about the illness.
One woman told me to beware of anyone who
sneezed or had a lump under their armpit or on
their thigh. That's how the sickness began, she said.

Another said the Great Pestilence killed a person from the inside out. You could smell death rotting the person's insides.

By the time I got home, I was tired. I was exhausted in my body and my heart. Everything felt so hopeless. I stepped inside my house and heard arguing. Papa and Paulo were sitting at the table. Papa's white hair caught the sunlight coming in from the open window. He turned and smiled at me.

"Hello, *piccolina*," he said.

"Hello, Papa," I said.

"What are we to do?" Paolo asked Papa, returning to their argument. "Stay and wait for the worst to happen?"

Papa glanced my way. "Let's not talk about this now. Maria is home."

"Are you talking about the funeral procession?" I asked. "I saw them when I returned the mending to the families."

"Which funeral procession? There are so many," said Paolo. "All we ever see or hear these days are funeral processions. One hundred people are dying every day."

"Paolo, stop!" Papa shouted. "You'll scare your sister."

"By telling her the truth?" Paolo asked. "She needs to know what's going on."

"She's a child," said Papa. "We must protect–"

"I already know all about it," I said quietly.

Papa and Paolo stopped talking. I sat at the table with them.

"Everyone's talking about the sickness," I said. "People are even making songs about it. Every time I step outside, there's someone to tell me a story."

"I don't like you going to market," said Papa. "Or taking in the mending. There are too many people with stories that aren't true. They sit and talk. You shouldn't listen."

"I'm not a child," I said. "I know what is happening. You don't know you're sick, not really sick, until you see the *bubo*," I said. I pointed to my upper thigh and then to my armpit. "It happens in one of these places. You wake up and there's a bump, a growth under your skin." My voice dropped to a whisper. "They say the bubo gurgles, that it talks to you."

Papa and Paolo glanced at each other.

I pushed my shoulders back and forced my voice to its normal volume. "You sneeze, and there's a rash. People say the illness kills you from the inside out, that you can smell the person dying." Tears started rolling down my cheeks. "They say it's a sign that the end of the world is here."

Papa pulled me onto his lap and hugged me tight. Tears were rolling down his cheeks too. "Shhh, piccolina. It will be all right," he said.

"No, it won't be, Papa," I sobbed. "Paolo is right. People are dying every day. The sickness is spreading. I'm scared it will take you, Nonna, Paolo and Joseph. And then I'll be all alone."

"It won't take any of us," said Papa. "The saints will protect us."

"The saints are in heaven, not on Earth," Paolo said. "We mustn't rely on them. We have to do something. We have to leave Florence."

"Running away won't help anyone," said Papa.

"We're not running. We're surviving," Paolo said. "Maria is right. The sickness is spreading and people are dying. I've heard the cities in the north aren't as sick. If we go, we can survive. We can't stay here and hope things get better!"

"Your ideas are madness," Papa said. "Flee to Milan? Why? You think the Great Pestilence will remain inside the walls of Florence? Stay here and listen to the doctors!"

"The doctors don't know anything," Paolo sneered. "They say the illness starts with the bubo. But I've heard that some people go to sleep and don't wake up."

Papa gave my brother a stern look. "The doctors know what they're doing," he said. "I trust them."

"What do we do while we wait for them to find a cure?" asked Paolo. "Pretend we don't hear the funeral bells? Pretend we don't hear our neighbours crying over their lost family?" He looked at me. "Do we pretend we don't smell death in the streets?"

"Paolo! Stop!" Papa's voice was tight and thin. He brushed the hair from my face. "You're scaring your sister!"

"Maria is already scared!" Paolo yelled. "We all are!"

With that, an angry silence filled the room. My body tightened. I wasn't sure who was right and who was wrong.

"We haven't any money," Papa said, the fight gone from his voice. "Even if we wanted to leave, we haven't enough money or food for the journey."

Paolo knelt in front of us. "Let me take the wool to Pisa and sell it. I can come back with money–"

"No! No!" Papa shook his head. "Don't even speak those words. If the guild found out that you were taking their wool–"

"Everyone is too busy trying to survive to notice if a little wool goes missing," said Paolo. "Hardly anyone is working anymore. They're too scared. We have to do what's right for us, Papa." He pointed at me. "We have to do what is right for Maria. Do you really want her to stay here?"

Papa kissed the top of my head. When he kissed my cheeks, I felt his tears on my skin. "No, no, I don't," he said to Paolo. He reached out and clutched Paolo's hand. "You are my children, my everything. I want you both to be safe."

"Then let me go," Paolo begged.

"It's too dangerous," Papa whispered.

"Papa, please," Paolo said, tears now running down his cheeks. "No one will know what I'm doing. Let me do this for our family. Let me do what I can to make sure we survive."

Papa was quiet for a moment. Then he nodded at Paolo. "Take the wool to Pisa," he said. "Sell it, not just for us, but so Joseph and Nonna can come with us too." Next, Papa turned to me. "Maria, go and tell Joseph that we're leaving the city in a few days. He and Nonna must prepare to come with us."

I jumped from his lap. He quickly pulled me back, his face very serious. "One more thing, piccolina," he said. "I trust Joseph and Nonna to keep a secret. But it's best to keep Paolo's plan to sell the wool between us. Don't tell anyone, not even our friends."

I nodded. "I understand." After I gave Papa and Paolo each a quick hug, I rushed out the door.

The sun was warming the day, but even its light couldn't shake the shadows that lingered on the streets. I grabbed a handful of weeds and spring wildflowers and held them close to my face. Then I ran to Joseph's house.

Joseph welcomed me inside and pulled the door closed tightly behind me. Nonna was at the table, drinking from a mug. Usually when I saw her, her dark eyes were bright with laughter. Today, however, they were clouded with sadness. She hadn't brushed her hair, and the grey strands stuck out at all angles.

"Maria," she said. "It is good to see you, child. How is the family?"

"We're doing well – for now," I said. I told her and Joseph of our plan to leave the city and take them along. I said we'd leave in a few days.

Nonna nodded. "I may be old, but I can do this," she said. "I must. I'm all the family Joseph has left.

I need to protect him." She reached out and took my hand. "Thank you for thinking of us."

"Where are you getting the money for the journey?" Joseph asked.

"Paolo has a plan," I said. "That's all I'm allowed to say."

Joseph nodded knowingly. "We'll be ready," he said.

I ran home and told my family that Joseph and Nonna would come with us.

"Good," Paolo said, hoisting a bag on his back. "I'll return as soon as I can." He hugged me tight, then did the same to Papa. Paolo walked out the door, and I closed it behind him.

"Now," said Papa, "we have work to do here." He showed me some coins. "It's not much, but it's all we have. You must sew the money into my clothing. We'll come home again, Maria, as soon as the sickness has passed. Let's not pack everything.

We'll bury or hide the important things for when we return."

I nodded.

"I must go to work and pretend as though nothing has changed," he said. "Can I trust you to do these things?"

I nodded again. "I won't let you down, Papa."

He smiled and squeezed my shoulder. "I know, piccolina."

We spent the next few days preparing. I sewed the few coins we had left into Papa's clothing. I buried or hid anything we didn't need for our journey. I woke up early and waited in the queue for bread. I did my mending jobs.

Four days after Paolo left for Pisa, Papa burst through the door. He was crying.

I dropped my sewing and jumped up. "Papa! What's happened?"

CHAPTER FOUR

"Papa! What is it? What's happened?" I asked again.

"Our city leaders," he said. "To protect us, they're making new rules."

"That's good," I said. "Anything that protects us is good, isn't it?"

Papa clutched my hands. "They're not allowing anyone from Genoa or Pisa to come into Florence."

The words took a minute to sink in. I wasn't sure I'd heard them right. "No one is allowed to come into Florence?" I repeated.

Papa was crying hard now. "Your brother," he said. "He can't come back home to us."

"What do you mean he can't come home?" I asked. My chest tightened. I couldn't breathe. "Of course, he can! We need him!"

"He can't! The new rule–!" Papa took a deep breath and caught me by the shoulders. "Our city leaders won't allow it."

"Then we must go to him, Papa," I said. "We can find him in Pisa. Then we can all go to Milan."

"We can't," Papa said. "The sickness has overtaken those cities." He wiped his eyes with his hands. "That is why no one from Genoa or Pisa can come here. Those cities have been destroyed by the sickness."

"But people here in Florence are already sick," I cried. "What does it matter?"

"It matters," Papa said. "The number of deaths is rising. If too many of us die of sickness, it will affect everything. There won't be food. There won't be work. There may not even be a city left anymore." He hugged me tightly. Tears streamed down his cheeks. "This is my fault! We should have gone with Paolo. Or I should have let him go sooner! What have I done?"

It was too much. Too much information about the new rules for Florence. Too many feelings about Paolo not being able to come home.

I couldn't believe Papa wouldn't agree that we should go and get him. My head was swimming. The world turned blurry. I pulled free from Papa and ran out the door.

"Maria! Come back!" he called.

I ran down the dusty road. The wind and tears stung my eyes. All around me were people dying. Their families had turned them out of their homes when they'd become sick. They lay on the sides of the road, groaning in pain and calling out for help.

Children, their mothers and fathers dead from the sickness, cried for their parents.

I couldn't help them. No one could. I ran all the way to Joseph's house.

When I got there, two men were coming out. They carried a body covered with a sheet. At that moment, my legs lost their strength. I fell to my knees and screamed.

"Maria!" a voice called.

I wiped away my tears and looked towards the house. Joseph was standing in the doorway. I scrambled to my feet and ran to him.

"Don't come any closer," he said, putting out his hand to stop me.

"He's right," said one of the men. "Best not to get too close."

I looked at the sheet-covered body they held between them.

"Nonna passed in the night," Joseph said.

"Was it the sickness?" I asked. I felt numb and cold. I had lost another person I loved.

"I don't know," Joseph said. "She didn't wake up this morning." He struggled to keep his voice steady. "Maybe it was old age."

"You can't stay here," I said. "You must come home with me."

"No," Joseph said, shaking his head.

He and I watched as the two men placed Nonna on the cart. She wasn't the only body on there. My throat tightened at the sight of them all.

"The men say there's a shortage of gravediggers," Joseph said.

It made sense. Who would want to touch the bodies of the dead? I shuddered at the thought. What if touching them meant you got sick too?

"They say a man can make a lot of money if he's willing to carry the bodies and bury them," Joseph continued.

"You can't," I said. "It's too dangerous!"

"No more dangerous than staying in the city and doing nothing or trying to leave." He pointed at the people shuffling down the road. "The sickness is everywhere, Maria. There's work to be done. And there's money to be made doing that work."

"What good is your money if you're dead?" I said. I made sure the men couldn't hear me, then I added, "Gravediggers aren't good people. They make families pay lots of money to take the bodies."

"They're not all bad," said Joseph. "Look around you. Look at all the bodies. Wouldn't you charge a high price if you had to do their work?"

"Please, don't do this! Come home with me," I said. "We'll take care of you."

"How?" he asked. "I heard what our city leaders said about people in Genoa and Pisa. Your brother can't come home. You don't have money." His voice softened. "I can't go with you, Maria. It will be hard enough for your father to get the two of you out of the city. You won't get far with another person in the group."

"Papa and I aren't leaving," I said. "Not until Paolo can come home." The tears fell down my cheeks. I had cried so much, I couldn't believe I still had tears to shed. "Please, Joseph. I don't know when I'll see Paolo again. I can't lose you too."

Joseph gave me a big smile. "You won't lose me. I'm too strong. Go and find Paolo, then go to Milan. When the sickness has passed, come back to Florence. You'll find me here. I promise."

I moved to give him a hug. But he jumped back and yelled.

"No, Maria! Don't touch me!"

CHAPTER **FIVE**

I froze in place.

"Don't touch me," Joseph said again, softer the second time. "We don't know why Nonna died. It could've been the sickness. We have to be careful."

It crushed me that I couldn't hug Joseph. "You're right," I said. "Take care."

"You too," he said. "I'll see you soon."

The people dying in the streets made the air smell of rot. I barely noticed it. I was too heartbroken at everything that had just happened.

Papa was waiting for me when I got home.

"Nonna died in the night," I said.

Tears fell from Papa's face.

"Joseph thinks she died of old age," I said. "But Paolo told me that sometimes the sickness takes people quietly."

"It's true," said Papa, wiping away the tears. "Sometimes people seem healthy. They go to sleep, but they never wake up." He put his hands together and raised them towards the ceiling. "I hope it was old age."

"I forgot to ask about the funeral," I said, feeling suddenly ashamed. I should have paid better attention. "I'll go back and find out."

"Piccolina," Papa said, putting his hand on my shoulder. "She's probably already buried. The mass graves, remember?"

People sharing graves. It was too terrible to think about. I looked out the window and saw the sun was setting. It felt as though darkness would spread until it took over all of Florence.

"Mass graves are the only way the city can keep up," said Papa. "The streets are being overrun by bodies."

I nodded. There was nothing to say.

"We must get Joseph and bring him here," Papa said. "He cannot be left alone."

"I tried, but he won't come," I said. "He is going to be a gravedigger."

"It is a death sentence," Papa whispered. "He will never survive."

"I told him that," I said. "He wouldn't listen. He says there's lots of money to be made digging graves. He says he's strong enough to survive the sickness."

"Maria, what have I done?" Papa clutched his hair. "If only I'd listened to Paolo months ago and got us out sooner."

"We can't help that now," I said, trying to make him feel better. "We must do what we can to survive."

"Yes, you're right," he said. He straightened his shoulders and pushed his hair away from his face. "We must leave for Milan. Is everything ready?"

"Leave? Papa, no, that's not what I meant! What about Paolo?" I said. "We can't go without him!"

Papa didn't answer me. But even in the shadows, I saw his head bow in sadness.

He doesn't think Paolo will ever come back, I thought. "Do you think he's–" I bit back the last words. I couldn't finish the thought.

"If anyone can survive this terrible disease, your brother can," said Papa.

I knew he was lying to make me feel better. "Can we go to Pisa and look for him? Instead of going to Milan?" I asked.

Papa shook his head. "It's too dangerous to go there," he said. "Your brother would never forgive me if I took you. And I would never forgive myself." Papa took my hands in his. "Florence isn't safe anymore," he said. "People think the world is ending. We can't stay here. It's too dangerous, especially for you."

I tried to understand what he was saying, but it was too much.

Suddenly, orange light poured through the open window. Papa and I ran to the window and stared outside. People were setting fires in the streets. Red and yellow flames rose into the darkening night.

"They're burning the clothing of the dead," said Papa. "It's another rule from our city leaders."

I watched smoke rise from the piles and wondered if the fires could put an end to the sickness. More and more clothing was added.

Soon the fires were burning brightly. They lit up the people lying sick and dying in the streets.

Just then a woman walked past our home, carrying a basket. Two men ran up to her. One of them grabbed her and held her tight. The other wrestled the basket from her hands. She cried out, struggling to free herself and get back her food. The men shoved her to the ground.

I shuddered. It seemed like the end of the world had truly come to Florence.

That's when my helplessness turned into anger. I couldn't watch and do nothing. I pushed past Papa and ran into the street.

"Get away from her!" I screamed.

I grabbed a stick from the ground and rushed at the men. They wrenched the basket from the woman, then ran away.

I dropped the stick and offered the woman my hand. "Can I help you up?" I asked her.

The woman wiped away tears. "Thank you," she said as I helped her to her feet.

"I'm sorry they stole your food," I said. "My papa and I don't have much, but you can come inside and—"

"Thank you," she said. "I'm not hungry anymore." She hung her head. Tears continued to run down her face.

"Do you want some water? Do you want to sit?" I asked.

The woman shook her head. "No, I have to get home," she said. She started walking away, then turned. "Thank you for your kindness," she said. "Thank you."

I nodded and went back inside.

Papa put his hands on my shoulders. "That was a dangerous thing to do," he told me. "But it was also the right thing to do. You are strong and brave, piccolina. I'm so proud of you."

Papa and I watched the fires and the people.

"You're right," I said after a while. "We can't wait for Paolo. And we can't go looking for him. We have to go to Milan."

The next morning, Papa packed wool he had stolen from the guild into his bag. I packed our small food supply into mine.

We started out of the city. Papa had been right about the sickness. It had taken over Florence. We were forced to step around the bodies in the road. I tried to say a prayer for each person I saw, but I soon lost my voice. Fires burned. A foul smell filled the air: a mix of rot, charred wood and dirt. Smoke burned my eyes and made me cough.

Something was different today though. I stopped and looked around.

"What is it?" asked Papa.

"The church bells," I said. "I can't hear them."

"Our city leaders have forbidden their ringing," said Papa. "They feel the sound is upsetting to those still left alive." He shook himself as though trying to cast off the words. "Keep going, piccolina. Just a little further and we'll be in the countryside, away from all of this." Papa smiled and pulled me close. His grip on my hand was tight. He scanned the faces of people passing us by, looking at them closely.

"Papa?" I asked as he watched a group of men coming towards us.

"Yes, I see them," Papa said. "Everything is fine. Let's go this way instead."

We turned left onto a smaller street. After a few steps, Papa looked back. His face tightened. The men were following us.

"It's a beautiful day," Papa said. "Walk faster so we can use all the sunlight."

"I know you want us to get away from the men, Papa," I said quietly.

He squeezed my hand. "I'm sorry you have to go through these hard days," he said. "But it is good you know what is going on." He jerked my hand, and we broke into a run.

Papa and I sped down the street. Suddenly, he twisted right.

"There!" He pointed to an empty house with its door open. "Get inside!"

We ran into the home, and Papa quickly closed the door behind us. Putting his finger to his lips, he crouched down. I knelt in a pool of shadows beneath the window and held my throbbing arm. I hoped the men would pass us by.

"Do you see them?" one of the men asked.

"No," said another, his voice hard and mean. "Who would think an old man and a child could move so quickly?"

"Forget them," said the first man. "Did you see their clothing? I bet they don't have anything worth taking anyway."

"Everyone has something worth taking," said the second man.

As he spoke, he moved closer and closer to the house. He stopped by the window.

I pressed my back against the wall and pushed my hand against my chest. My heart beat so hard that I heard it in my ears. I wanted to scream and run. But I forced myself to stay still.

CHAPTER SIX

"Let's go," said the first man after a moment.

I heard the group walk away. I started to stand, but Papa reached out and held me still.

"Wait," he whispered. "Sometimes they hide."

I stayed still, even though insects crawled from the dirt floor onto my legs. I didn't dare brush them off. I was scared of making noise. The insects kept coming. Soon they were climbing onto my chest and shoulders, buzzing around my ears. Mice scurried from the shadows and darted across the floor.

I wanted to crawl out of my skin! I wanted to scream, to shake off the insects and run as fast and as far as I could. I pressed my hands against my mouth and forced myself not to cry out. The sun rose and cast its light into the house. Dirty clothing was balled into a pile. The bed had been overturned.

"It's good," Papa said, rising slowly and peering out the window. "They've gone."

I leapt to my feet and brushed the insects off my skin and hair.

Papa opened the door, just a crack, and looked out. "Let's go."

The two of us walked quickly. To be safe, we took a twisting, winding route, staying away from most of the crowds on the main streets. As we passed by one house, we saw Joseph! He and another man were hauling a dead body. They placed it onto their cart. A gust of wind sent dust and dirt from the dead person's clothing right into Joseph's face. He coughed, turned, and saw us.

Papa and I stopped and waved. I took a step, wanting to run to Joseph. But Papa caught my arm and pulled me back. He met my eyes and gave me a small shake of his head.

Joseph smiled and lifted his hand in hello.

He looked tired and worn down. More than that, he was pale and moving slowly. I knew then that this would be the last time I saw him. He would be dead from the Great Pestilence soon.

I was losing everything and everyone, all at once. A scream started inside me. I felt it pushing its way up, ready to explode. But I knew our survival depended on not giving into my terrible sadness. I shoved down all the bad feelings and locked them away in a dark place in the pit of my stomach.

For the next few days, I pushed all thoughts of Joseph, Nonna and Paolo out of my head. Sometimes, that was easy to do. The roads were rocky and dusty, and it took all of my strength to walk all day. I didn't have energy to think. Papa and I tried to ration food. Soon, all that was left to eat was grass and weeds.

One day, we came upon a farm. No one was there. Papa and I went into the house and found bread, nuts and some beans.

"The family must have left recently," said Papa. He packed the food into his bag.

"Papa, look," I said. I held up a small bit of cheese for him to see. "How did they have money for this?"

"They probably stole it," he said. "Look at us, piccolina. We are rooting through their empty home, searching for anything to eat. They probably did the same thing, but in a wealthier home."

"Should we do this?" I asked. "Should we take food that isn't ours?"

"It was wrong for your brother and me to steal wool. And, yes, it is wrong to take food that doesn't belong to us," Papa said sadly. "But we must do what we can to survive. The people who once lived here are gone. Any food they left behind is fine for us to take. If they had needed the food, they would have packed it up with them."

With that, Papa put the cheese in his bag, and we continued on our journey.

That night, I cried with joy at finally having food in my belly. But later, by the fire, I cried different tears. Not worrying about hunger meant I could finally think of Mamma, Flora, Paolo, Joseph and Nonna.

I rolled away from Papa, so he wouldn't see my tears. His breathing slowed as he fell asleep. I added more branches to the fire. The stars

were bright in the sky before I finally fell into a dreamless sleep.

The next morning, I woke to snuffling sounds. Something soft and wet nuzzled my neck. My eyes snapped open, and I found myself looking into the bright brown eyes of a young, female dog. She was small, with brown and black patches.

"Papa!" I said.

Papa sat up and rubbed his eyes. "What is it, Maria? What is that?"

"A dog," I said happily.

She licked my nose, and I giggled. Her tongue tickled.

"Run it off," said Papa. "We can't feed another mouth."

"But she came to us," I said. "We can't turn her away."

"She didn't come to us," Papa argued. "She came to the fire. She wanted to be warm. That's all."

"She wanted company," I said. "If all she wanted was the fire, she would be gone by now." I pointed at the cold embers. "The fire's dead."

Papa stood and stretched. "It doesn't matter. Run it off." He picked up a rock to throw at the dog's paws.

"Stop it!" I yelled. "Don't hurt her!"

"I only want her to leave," Papa said. "I don't want to hurt her. We just don't have enough food for three of us."

"I don't care," I said, climbing to my feet. "We couldn't help the people on the street. We couldn't help Mamma, Flora, Paolo, Nonna or Joseph." I stood between Papa and the dog. "I'm not leaving anyone else. I don't care if we can help her only for a day. We're going to help her. We're going to help *someone*!"

Papa raised his eyebrows and his hands. "Fine," he said. He sounded annoyed, but there was a twinkle in his eye. "The dog comes with us. We can't call her 'dog' though. She needs a proper name."

"I already have one," I said, rubbing her head. "Speranza."

"Speranza," Papa said thoughtfully. "I like it. We could use a little hope."

There was something about having Speranza that turned the next few days brighter and lighter. Maybe it was because she always seemed to find a reason to be happy. She made the road seem smoother. Papa and I were glad for her company.

"I'll say this," said Papa a couple days later. "Speranza has paid her way."

It was true. Thanks to her excellent hunting, we'd been eating rabbits and birds. She wandered during her hunts, following the animal scents.

Sometimes I followed her, and I was able to find berries and plants. "She is small but fierce," I said.

"Just like you," Papa laughed. "Her bark is twice the size of her. She's also doing a great job of warning of us of bandits on the road." He bent down and scratched her face. "You are a very good dog."

That night, Papa found us a circle of trees. They protected us from the wind. He built us a fire and cooked us dinner. Then we settled in for the night.

"We'll be in Milan tomorrow," said Papa. "When we get settled, we'll find a way to get a message to Paolo. If he's still alive, we'll bring him home." He kissed the top of my head, then turned away to sleep.

"One more day," I told Speranza, cuddling her close. "One more day, and it will all be over."

Late that night, I woke to Papa crying. I opened my eyes and sat up. He was kneeling by the fire,

hands tucked into his armpits. Tears fell down his
cheeks.

"Papa?" I said. "What is it? Did you have a bad
dream?"

He looked at me. "I'm sorry, piccolina," he said.
"I woke up because I thought I was sleeping on
a rock." His tears fell harder and faster. "But it's
no rock. It's a bubo. I'm infected."

CHAPTER SEVEN

"No! Are you sure?" I asked, my stomach clenching. The food inside it tossed and turned. I swallowed hard to keep everything down.

Papa nodded. "It's here." He lifted his hand and gently touched a spot under his left armpit.

"What should we do?" I glanced around for a softer place for him to sleep. Everywhere I looked, the ground was hard. "I can go back to the farm and bring blankets. It's a half-day's journey, but–"

Papa raised his hand to stop me. "Piccolina," he said, "we both know what this means." He paused and looked at me with such love, I wanted to cry. "You must go on without me," he said.

"Papa, no! I can't leave you!"

"You must!" His voice was stern. "You cannot be here."

"I can't leave you alone," I said. "That would be wrong."

"It would be wrong for you to be here," he replied. "We had a plan to go to Milan. You must do it for us."

When I didn't say anything, Papa continued, "Take Speranza. She'll protect you as you travel north. It's just a day's walk. Stay off the main road but close to it so you don't get lost."

"Maybe it's an insect bite," I said. I refused to believe what he was saying.

Papa gave me a sad smile. "It's not a bite." Softly, he continued, "I don't want you to see me getting sicker. Please, go."

"At least let me stay until you–" I caught my breath. "Let me stay until the end."

He shook his head. "No, I'm your father. It's up to me to protect you and to protect the other people travelling to Milan. I need to go deep into the woods, to stay away from everyone and keep them safe." He took a deep breath and exhaled. "Let me do this last thing for you, piccolina. Let me be your papa, one last time."

I jumped up and rushed to hug him. But Papa scrambled backwards, just as Joseph had after Nonna died.

"No, it's best not to touch me," Papa said.

I sank to my knees. Speranza whined softly and inched my way.

Papa ripped the coins from his clothing and threw them to me.

"It's not much," he said. "I'm sorry I couldn't give you more."

"You're my papa," I said. I tried to keep my voice strong so he wouldn't know how badly I hurt. "You're all I need."

He nodded at the coins. I picked them up and hid them in my shoes.

Papa and I didn't sleep the rest of the night. We sat opposite each other and let the fire keep us warm. When the sun rose, he pointed at the road. "I promise you," he said, "if I get better, I will come and find you."

"I love you, Papa," I said. I stared at him and tried not to cry. I promised myself I would always remember the kindness in his eyes. I would remember the way the wind lifted his hair and the love in his smile.

"I love you too, piccolina," he said. "I love you forever."

I picked up my bag and left with Speranza by my side. Once I was out of his sight, though,

I couldn't stand it anymore. I dropped to my knees and let the tears fall. My body shuddered until I thought my bones would rattle loose. I'd lost everyone I'd ever loved.

Speranza nudged my arm.

I took a deep breath and wiped away the tears. "We have to go back, girl," I told her. "Quietly, so Papa doesn't know we're there. We have to be with him until the end." I picked my way through the trees, then quietly made my way back.

When I got closer, I saw Papa doubled over. Sobs wracked his body. I watched him for a moment. *It would have been easy for him to ask me to stay*, I thought. *He told me to leave so I wouldn't see him like this. He told me to leave so I wouldn't get sick too.*

I sat down. Even though Papa couldn't see or hear me, I cried silently with him. I cried until my eyes felt puffy and dry. I cried until my head throbbed.

After a while, Papa got up and moved deeper into the forest. Soon, I lost him in the shadows.

He's giving up everything to keep me and all the other travellers safe, I realized. I wiped my eyes. If my father was strong enough to do this, I would be strong too. I would honour his last wish and go to Milan.

The rest of the day, I stayed off the main path. Speranza and I moved carefully through the roots and brambles. The morning's fog and chill gave way to the warm air of spring. The air was sweet and clean. I heard the chirping of birds.

"Maybe we'll lay a trap for one of them and eat well tonight," I said to Speranza. "Or maybe we'll follow the birds. They'll know where water, berries and plants will be."

As morning became afternoon, more and more travellers filled the road. I stayed out of their sight. One of the groups had children. I heard them singing. Their voices carried in the wind, and I caught every word. They were singing a song about the sickness.

"Ring around the rosie," they sang, "a pocketful of posy."

That part was about the rash that appeared on people's skin. It was also about the flowers and herbs we carried near our faces to stop the smell of the sickness.

"Achoo, achoo, we all fall down!" all the children sang.

"That's how Papa will pass," I told Speranza. "Sneezes and chills. Then he'll–" I stopped, then leaned against a tree. I couldn't bear to think of how Papa would die. I couldn't bear to hear the children singing about it. I sat down and waited until they were too far for me to hear them anymore.

Speranza and I started on our path again. I passed the time by telling her stories of Mamma,

Flora, Papa, Paolo, Joseph and Nonna. It hurt to talk about them. At the same time, it felt good to remember my family.

Papa had thought it would take a day to get to Milan. But since Speranza and I weren't using the road, it was taking longer.

"We'll have to settle in for one more night," I told Speranza.

She chuffed and wagged her tail.

As the sun set, I searched for flat ground with some protection from the wind. I gathered sticks for a fire. Speranza made me laugh by stealing them and dancing away.

"Come on, silly girl," I said, grabbing the branch in her mouth. "Let it go."

She shook her head, held on and pulled. She playfully growled.

I giggled and wrestled with her for the branch. It felt good to laugh again. After I finally got the branch from her, I lit the fire. We settled in for the night.

"What would you like for dinner? I have bread from the farmhouse, cheese and–"

Speranza suddenly jumped into the bushes. She rustled around, then came out a moment later carrying a bird in her mouth.

"Got it," I smiled. "You'll take care of your own dinner."

After we ate, we curled closer to the fire. To keep the coins safe, I buried them in the ground, close to the flames. Just as I was falling asleep, I felt Speranza leave my side. I heard the sound of twigs breaking.

"Another bird?" I asked my dog sleepily.

I opened my eyes and saw the hairs on the back of Speranza's neck rise. She bared her teeth and dropped her shoulders. A low, angry growl rolled from her throat.

Out of the shadows came a group of three men.

I scrambled to the fire and snatched a burning branch. Holding it like a torch, I took a closer look at the men.

The biggest one, with blonde hair and a beard, rubbed his hands and came towards me. "Well, well, well," he said. "What do we have here?"

Speranza growled again and came closer to protect me.

The men laughed. It was an evil sound.

I stepped in front of Speranza.

"Don't worry," said the bearded man, smiling dangerously. "We won't hurt you or your dog." He stepped closer. "As long as you give us what we want."

CHAPTER **EIGHT**

15 April 1348
On the road to Milan, Italy

I backed away from the men, keeping my torch high and the fire between us. My heart hammered in my chest. My legs felt weak, but I kept a fierce look on my face. I hoped the men couldn't see my body shaking.

"Come, girl," said a short man with darker hair. "No need to be upset. Give us what we want, and we'll be on our way."

"What – what do you want?" I glanced down at Speranza. She was all I had in the world. I wouldn't let them take her from me.

"Keep your mutt," said the man. He pointed at the hem of my dress. "Give us the coins you've got sewn into your dress."

"I don't have any coins sewn into my dress," I told them. It was true. The coins were buried in the dirt. I knew the men wouldn't leave me alone, whether I gave them the money or not. "I promise. I have no money in my dress."

My words made the man laugh.

"A little girl on her own in the night, in the middle of the woods?" he asked. "You wouldn't set out alone if you didn't have money."

The bearded man pushed him. "Don't be foolish. Everyone is dying. People are fleeing." He knelt by the fire and put out his hands. "Did you hear of what's happening in the world, little one? Do you know they've begun walling the sick inside their homes?"

The tall, thin man spoke for the first time. "Not just the sick," he said. "Everyone is being walled inside, whether they are sick or not. As soon as the neighbours know one person in a house is sick, they wall up everyone."

It was too horrible to think about. I pressed my hand against my mouth so I wouldn't scream.

"Now, now, don't frighten the child by telling her such tales," said the bearded man. He smiled at me. But it wasn't a nice smile. It wasn't meant to comfort. It was a warning.

"The world is ending, little one," he continued. "It's time for each of us to take care of ourselves. Laws no longer matter. Friendships and family no longer matter. The only thing that matters is money and what it can buy. Understand?" He stood and dusted his hands. "Give us the coins in your dress, and we'll be on our way."

"I swear, I haven't anything in my dress," I said, my voice shaking.

"Perhaps it's elsewhere," said the thin man.

Out of the corner of my eye, I saw Speranza tighten every muscle she had.

"Maybe it's in her shoes," the thin man continued. "Or maybe it's – *here*."

The thin man grabbed for my bag. As soon as he did, Speranza launched herself at him. Her jaws clamped down hard on his leg. The thin man howled in pain.

Speranza leapt back, readying for another round. The hairs on her neck and back stood high.

"Stupid mutt," the thin man said. He lifted his good leg to kick her.

I jumped in front of him and shoved the torch at his stomach. He roared in fear and stumbled back.

The bearded man laughed. "The little one and her guard dog have spirit," he said. Then his laughter disappeared, and his face hardened. "I'm finished with games. Give me what I want before I hurt you both."

I stood tall. "Hurt my dog, and I will hurt you more," I said. I had lost my entire family. I refused to lose Speranza. She was all I had. These men wouldn't take her from me, and I wouldn't let them take the only money we had to survive. Paolo and Papa had given up everything to keep me safe. I wasn't about to surrender.

His eyebrows went up. "You think so, hmm?"

"I promise you." I took another burning branch from the fire and readied for the fight.

CHAPTER **NINE**

15 April 1348
On the road to Milan, Italy

Suddenly, voices came from the road. They were joined by the creak of cart wheels and banging of metal objects rattling around in the cart. A group of women, children and men saw Speranza and me and stopped. The adults looked between me and the three men. A hard, protective light came into their faces. They moved towards me.

The bandits stumbled backwards.

The women and men carried torches. The leader of the group was a strongly built woman with black hair.

"What do we have here?" she asked the bandits.

"Nothing that concerns you," said the bearded man. "A little quarrel between me and my niece."

The woman turned to me. "Is that true, girl? Is he your family?"

"He is no family of mine," I said. "None of them are."

"It's time for you to be off," the woman said to the bandits. "Be off, before you regret this night."

The bearded man smiled. He looked at the group of people behind her. There were six adults and four children. The bearded man and his friends were outnumbered. He tipped his head towards me. Then the three men disappeared into the forest.

I wanted to thank the woman and her group. But they stood, tight and frozen, watching the men. When all sound faded, the woman relaxed. She turned and held out her hand to Speranza. The hairs on Speranza's neck and back went down. She sat and wagged her tail. "Yes, I think they've gone too," the woman said to my dog.

The woman turned to me. "You're safe now, little one. Sometimes the men hide in the darkness and wait for travellers to fall asleep. You're wise to journey with the dog."

"Speranza," I said, finding my voice. "Her name is Speranza."

"A good name for a good dog," the woman said. "My name is Flipipa Cosimo. I travel with my aunt, her child and those we have found on our way."

"Helped," said an old woman in the group. "She didn't just find us; she's helped us too."

"We help each other," said Flipipa. "These are hard times. They are made easier when we offer kindness."

Speranza came close to me and nosed my leg. I dropped to her, held her close and threaded my fingers in her wiry hair. My legs and hands

trembled. My stomach rolled. I took deep breaths, trying to calm the shaking and the sick feeling.

"Come," said Flipipa softly. "What is your name?"

"Maria," I said. "Maria Rosso."

"And where are your people?" She frowned into the darkness. "Have you been travelling to Milan on your own?"

I shook my head. "No, it was my papa and me. He took ill yesterday. I think he is dying. He promised to find me if he felt better and–" It was all I could get out. The danger of the bandits and losing my papa were too much. I couldn't breathe. I couldn't think. All I could do was sob.

"Good, good," Flipipa said. "Cry your tears. Take your breaths."

I wept as I told the group about all the family I had lost. They listened, offering their own stories. The old woman had been left alone by her son.

Most of the children had lost their parents to the sickness. Two of the men had woken one morning to find their wives gone.

Flipipa's husband was a merchant who got sick and died. "I promised him I would take our family to Milan," she said. "It would have been faster if we didn't have to walk. But these times call for caution." She gestured to her worn dress. "It's dangerous to show any sign of wealth."

I nodded, thinking that the bandits had been willing to hurt me and Speranza for just a few coins.

The men in Flipipa's group tended the fire. Soon it was hot and burning brightly. The adults put meat on a stick and roasted dinner.

"You will eat with us," said Flipipa. "You and Speranza will stay with us too. We will keep you safe until your papa can find you." She held me close. "And if he is gone, child, we will keep you safe until you're grown."

"Thank you," I gasped and clung to her.

"Thank you."

The next morning, we set out for Milan.
I stayed in the centre of the group. I didn't say
much, just let the voices of my new friends wash
over me. The smaller children played with Speranza,
and her happy barks brightened the day. I kept up
with Flipipa, but I couldn't help looking over my
shoulder and hoping to see Papa.

CHAPTER TEN

I stood in the doorway of the house Flipipa had bought when we settled in Milan five months ago. The sickness was still here, but things were slowly returning to normal.

Because of the Great Pestilence, all the clothing of the dead had to be burned. As a result, there was a high demand for fabrics, wool and clothing. With Flipipa's help, I had sold Papa's stolen wool shortly after we reached Milan. I had offered the money to Flipipa in return for boarding and food. She had refused.

"Pay back the kindness others have shown you with more kindness," she had said. "That will be payment enough for me."

Today's morning breeze carried the promise of warmth, sunshine and sweet air. I wrapped my arms around myself and leaned against the door frame.

"Are you going to see your family?" Flipipa asked as she came to stand beside me.

I nodded and smiled.

Flipipa handed me some pink flowers. "For them," she said.

I hugged her and called to Speranza, "Let's go!"

Two dogs came running, Speranza and Gioia. The day we entered Milan, I'd found Gioia on the outskirts of the city. He was a tiny grey and white puppy then. These days, he reached my hips. As big as he was though, Speranza was the boss of the two. She nipped at Gioia's hind legs, then trotted outside. Gioia chuffed and followed after her.

The dogs and I made our way through the field. A large, leafy tree marked the spot I'd chosen to put crosses to remember my family. Yesterday, I'd put the crosses in place.

It had been hard work, not only physically, but also emotionally. With each cross, I had remembered the person, the love and the memories. By the time I had finished, I was exhausted, and my vision was blurry from sweat and tears. I hadn't the energy to talk to my family yesterday. That's what I was going to do today.

"Hello, Papa," I said, standing in front of the first cross. My voice caught in my throat as his face came to my mind. I remembered his smile and the love in the way he used to say my name. I laid a flower at the base of the cross.

"Hello, Paolo," I said, laying a flower at the second cross. I took a deep breath and remembered my brother's laughter and the way he protected me.

Then I moved to the crosses I had made for Joseph, Nonna, Mamma and Flora. I laid flowers at each one. I thought of the holes my loved ones had left behind. I would never again run through the streets with Joseph, never make bread with Nonna. I'd never hug Mamma or watch Flora grow up. It was hard to think of these things. The loss left me gasping for breath.

Flipipa said that while the hurt would never go away completely, it would fade in time. One day, she promised me, the sadness wouldn't outweigh the happiness of the remembering.

"The Great Pestilence is leaving now," I said, speaking to the crosses. "People are returning to their homes. The cities are rebuilding."

Flipipa had done her best to search for news of my family members, if they might still be alive. When that failed, we tried to find where they might have been buried. But the pestilence had done its terrible work. Too many people had died and been buried in mass graves. It meant I would never find where my family's bodies lay.

Some days, I still couldn't believe they were gone. Some days I expected to see them walk through Flipipa's door. There were many nights when I dreamed they were still alive.

"We picked berries from the field," I said aloud. "I'm going to make jam to sell at the market." I ran my hand along Papa's cross. "Flipipa says because so many workers died, I'll be able to get higher pay when I decide to work. I don't know what I'll do yet. Flipipa says I don't have to rush. I can take my time. If I want, she'll employ a tutor for me." I paused, thinking of what that meant. "Maybe I won't have to work for a family or in a shop, Papa. Maybe I'll be a teacher."

The tears came, and I didn't bother to wipe them away. "Thank you for keeping me safe all of those years," I said to my family. "Thank you for all the happiness and love you gave me. I promise I will live my life to its very best to honour you and your love." I touched each of the crosses. Then I called the dogs to me and headed back home to help Flipipa with the day's chores.

A NOTE FROM THE AUTHOR

When it came to writing a story about the Great
Pestilence, balancing fact and fiction was one of my
most important tasks. The people of Florence had
suffered through earthquakes, economic catastrophes
and too much rain. All of it had added to a low-growth
season, which led to severe food shortages. Research
suggests that by Easter of 1347, bread was being
rationed to 94,000 people, with 4,000 Florentines dying
of malnutrition. People, much like Maria, were forced
to eat grass and weeds. It was a hard time, but the spirit
of the people was strong. I wanted to be sure to honour
those whose story I was telling and to do my best to tell
it correctly.

Sometimes, I found this task difficult. To be sure,
there were facts that couldn't be denied. The plague
devastated the city of Florence. But did it enter the
city via a boat full of infected soldiers? No. Research
suggests a change in the wind's direction pushed the

virus inland. However, there were stories of other cities firing arrows at infected ships. This was one of the places where fact and fiction blurred in the telling of Maria's story.

It was a similar process with the characters and what I imagined was happening at the time. Much of the information, especially for those in the lower class, would have spread via word of mouth. Facts could get lost. So, was it possible that while Paolo knew of the devastation of Genoa, he didn't know about Pisa? Maybe. Was it probable that in his desperation to take care of his family, he knew of Pisa but ignored the risks in order to make money they needed? Yes, I think so. I believe there were many people who put their lives on the line and stepped into dangerous situations. They were desperate to take care of their families.

I loved creating the character of Maria, imagining the life she would have had and cheering her on through the story. As a girl living in the 1300s, she would not have had the same freedoms and choices that girls today have. Indeed, as a poor girl of the lower class, many options would have been out of her reach. But there, again, was the mixing of fact and fiction. How much education would she have been granted? It seems likely she would have been taught basic skills such as reading, though unlikely she would have been taught maths. Would she have been able to become a teacher and been able to teach girls? I don't know. But I like to think so.

I like to think Maria lived to an old age, surrounded by loving family and friends. I daydream that Paolo survived and eventually found Maria.

That is the beauty of storytelling. It allows us to dream, to create hope in hard times, to see kindness amidst fear. In dreaming of a happy ending for Maria, I am able to dream of happy endings for us all. No matter your troubles, I hope you never stop dreaming, and never stop hoping for your happy ending.

GLOSSARY

gioia Italian word for "joy"

guild strictly controlled group of merchants or craftspeople, especially before the year 1500, who worked in the same trade; to become a guild member, one had to learn a trade and pay to study under a master

infect cause disease or illness

mourner person who shows sadness or loss at another person's death

pestilence illness; specifically refers to sicknesses that cause death

piccolina Italian word for "little one"

procession group of people moving in an orderly way

ration limit to keep from running out

speranza Italian word for "hope"

MAKING CONNECTIONS

1. In Chapter Three, Papa and Paolo argue over Paolo taking wool and selling it. Later, in Chapter Six, Maria and Papa talk about whether it's right to take food from the farmhouse. Is it always wrong to take something that doesn't belong to you? Or do you think Papa and Maria did what they had to do to survive? Explain your answer.

2. Flipipa finds Maria and Speranza in the woods. If Flipipa hadn't included Maria in her group, and Maria had gone to Milan alone, what do you think her life would have been like? What do you think she would've done to survive?

3. Maria loses her family and friends to the plague, but she is hopeful at the end of the story. How do you think the experiences she had as a child will affect her as she becomes an adult?

ABOUT THE AUTHOR

Natasha Deen graduated from college with a
psychology degree, but her passion has always revolved
around stories. She has written mysteries, action,
historical and fantasy novels for kids, teens and adults.
For her, one of the best things about being an author is
the chance to slip into other times and worlds, and to be
anything she can imagine through her characters. Natasha
lives in Alberta, Canada, with her pets and husband.
When she's not writing, she spends a lot of time trying to
convince her animals that she's the real boss of the house.